This book belongs to

_____

_____

Aged _____

STORIES FOR THE YOUNG READER

THE
Smallest Giant

AND OTHER STORIES

THE
Smallest Giant

AND OTHER STORIES

p

This is a Parragon Book
This edition published in 2002

Parragon
Queen Street House
4 Queen Street
Bath BA1 1HE, UK

ISBN 0-75258-420-0

Designed by Mik Martin

Printed in Italy

These stories have been previously
published by Parragon in the
Bumper Bedtime Series

CONTENTS

The Smallest Giant

Written by Dave King

ALBERT THE GIANT had a big
problem. Or rather, he had a
little problem that was, in
fact, a big problem! And if all that
sounds a trifle confusing, imagine
how poor Albert felt.

Albert's problem was this: he
wasn't a very big giant.

Now, if you or I were to look at
Albert, we would definitely say he
was a big giant. Certainly, if you
were to invite him round for tea at
your house, you would soon see
how big Albert was when he
couldn't get in through the front
door in fact, he'd probably be taller
than your entire house.

But in the Land of the Giants (a

place not too far from the Land of the Pixies and just to the right of Fairyland —you can't miss it because it's well signposted from the motorway) there were some really, really, really tall giants. These were not the kind of giants you would choose to pick a fight with, as you might end up with a sore nose (unless, of course, you happen to be an even taller giant).

So, although Albert was undeniably a giant, in comparison to most of his friends he was a very short giant indeed!

As you can imagine, this led to one or two problems for Albert. Some of the other, taller giants would tease Albert. "Ha!" they would say. "Call yourself a giant — a giant elf maybe! Perhaps you should go and live in the Land of the Pixies, with all the other little people!"

Albert would hang his head in shame. This kind of talk made him feel very sad, and sometimes a big fat tear would roll down his cheek. He wished he could be the same size as all the others and he had tried all sorts of things to make himself grow.

He had even visited a wise old witch in Fairyland, but the spell she gave him just made his nose grow longer and longer, so he'd had to go back and get the spell reversed. But generally speaking, he was a happy giant, and he did his best to keep cheerful about things.

One day, Albert was sitting at home reading a copy of *Gnomes and Gardens* magazine — a publication that delved into the lives and

homes of gnomes, elves, pixies, fairies, sprites and all manner of little, magical people. It was a favourite of Albert's, as reading about people smaller than himself usually made him feel really rather tall. Suddenly, he heard a dreadful commotion coming from outside his house.

He rushed over to the window only to discover that his view was blocked by masses of other giants, out in the street.

He tore open the front door and tried to push his way through the crowd. "Excuse me!" he shouted."What's going on? What are you all looking at?"

But it was no use. The crowd of giants, with their backs to Albert, were cheering too loudly. If you've ever heard one giant shout, you're probably deaf by now! Just imagine how loud a whole crowd of giants can be … loud enough to knock your next door neighbour's wig off, I'll guarantee!

Whatever was happening in the middle of the street, it was making the giants very excited. Albert didn't want to miss all the fun, so he dropped down onto his hands and knees and began to weave his way between the legs of the crowd. After a while he reached the front of the crowd, and through the tangle of legs he could see a big crowd on the other side of the street, equally excited and equally noisy.

Albert tilted his head to one side and listened. Just above the roar of the crowd he could hear something. It sounded like ... it was ... yes, Albert could definitely hear the sound of a trumpet! He wiggled through the rest of the crowd and stood up. The sight that greeted him as he looked down the street was a grand one. Smiling regally from inside his royal carriage, the King of the Giants was leading a grand parade through the streets of the town. It was the tenth anniversary of the King's coronation, and he was leading the way to an enormous party being held in his honour.

The King was a real sight to see, bedecked in jewels from top to toe and with a gleaming crown. "I bet that cost him a few week's pocket money!" Albert thought, as he stared at the King's finery.

Now it just so happened that for the past few weeks, King Bill the Second had been on a diet. He was rather fond of food, to say the least.

It was nothing for him to eat two chickens, a raspberry trifle, a plate of chips, three doughnuts and a chocolate fudge cake all in one go. And that was just for breakfast!

"You must get some exercise, and lose some weight!" Doctor Harold, the Royal Physician had told him. "And if I might suggest..." the doctor continued, holding up a videotape, "I've just brought out my own exercise tape, Lose Weight the

Harold Way! Only nine pounds, ninety nine pence to you, Sire!"

Even after the doctor had been thrown out into the street, the medical man's words rang true in the King's ears as he looked down at his flabby waist. He decided to go on a diet, cutting down on all the cakes and sweets that he liked to munch on during his favourite television shows, eating more sensibly and even taking a little, just a little, mind . . . exercise.

And so it was that just as King Bill drew near to where Albert was standing, he gave one of his little royal waves (which he was frightfully good at), and as he did so, one of his most beautiful — and horrendously expensive — rings slid off his newly slender finger, landing with a clink in the road and rolling several yards before sliding straight down a drain grating!

"It's disappeared, your Highness." said one of the King's guards, scratching his head and peering down the drain. "We'll never get it out of there!"

The King let out a terrible shriek. "My ring!" he cried. "Oh woe! Truly my ring is lost for ever!" Albert thought the King was over-reacting a bit. He watched as the other giants took turns to try and pull the grate up from the drain.

They huffed and they puffed, but try as they might, it just wouldn't budge.

"There will be no more festivities until my ring is found," declared the King.

Albert decided it was time to help out. "Um . . . excuse me, I'm sorry to bother you, your Majesty, but I think I might be able to help!" Albert said politely (he was a particularly polite giant, you see).

King Bill looked down his long, regal nose at Albert. "You?" he said, snootily. "But you're only a little giant! How can you possibly help?"

Without answering, Albert squeezed his small arm through the grate and, after a bit of puffing and grunting (although it might have been a bit of grunting and puffing, you can never be sure in cases like these), he pulled out the King's ring!

The King snatched his ring, and without a word of thanks, waved his carriage on down the street with more than a dash of pomp. This was a very rude thing for the King to do, certainly, but king's are like that sometimes. More importantly, however, all the other giants saw what Albert had done, and lifting him high on their shoulders, cheered louder than ever because Albert had saved the day.

The party lasted all night, and from that day forward no one ever teased Albert about being small again!

The Lost Giant

Written by Amber Hunt

THE AIR wobbled a bit, shimmered, swirled and with a 'whoomph' a rather bewildered, twelve-foot giant appeared. He was only a very young giant, and looked rather like any other young boy-except he was slightly larger, of course!

"Oh dear," said the giant, stepping on a bush and flattening it. Turning round he bumped into a tree, which bent over at an alarming angle.

"Hello," said a tiny voice.

"What was that?!" said the giant, startled. He whirled round looking for the voice and knocked the tree right over. "Where am I?"

"Stand still," yelled the small voice. "You're in our farmyard. I suspect you are all my fault!"

"Pardon?" said the giant. "Did you say I'm all your fault?"

"Yes," yelled the small voice,

"Only could you whisper because you are deafening me."

"Of course," apologised the giant and stepping back he trod in the pond and got his socks wet.

"Stand still please, before you demolish the whole farmyard," pleaded the voice.

"Where are you?" asked the giant.

"I'm down here, by the well. Perhaps if you bend down, carefully, you might be able to see me."

And so, carefully, the giant bent down and peered at the well. Standing next to it was a little boy with blond hair and very dirty knees.

"Oh," said the giant. "You're a little boy ... aren't you afraid of me? All the little boys in my story books are afraid of giants."

"No, I'm not afraid," said the little boy.

The giant got down on his hands and knees to get a closer

look. "Gosh, your knees are dirty," he said. "Have you been playing?"

The little boy looked at his knees. "Um, yes, I suppose they are a bit dirty. I lost my magic marble and was crawling around looking for it. This is a farmyard you know, so it gets a bit muddy."

"Oh," breathed the giant. "Have you got a magic marble? I've got one too. Here look," and he fished a marble as big as a doughnut out of his pocket.

"Wow," said the little boy. "That's wonderful. I wish I could find mine." Then a thought crossed his mind. "How old are you?" he asked the giant.

"Seventy," replied the giant.

"Oh," said the little boy, clearly disappointed.

"But I think ten giant years are the same as one of your years, so I suppose I'm about seven in your world."

"I'm seven too!" said the little boy. "That's terrific! You know what, I think my marble magicked you here. I was wishing for someone to play with when the air went wobbly. I was so scared I dropped my marble, which was why I was crawling around in the mud looking for it — and then you appeared. What's your name?" he asked. "Mine's Oliver."

"I'm Bertie," said the giant. "I was wishing for a friend on my marble too," and they looked at each other in awe.

"Wow," they breathed together. "Weird!"

Just then a voice called from inside the farmhouse, "Oliver, Oliver!"

"Oh no," said Oliver, "that's my mum. You'd better hide quickly." Oliver looked at his large friend. Where on earth do you hide a twelve-foot giant?

"I've got it," he said, "in the barn. Follow me — very carefully."

Oliver ran across the yard, with Bertie following — carefully. They went down past the stables, across the cornfield and into the meadow where the hay barn was.

"Oliver, Oliver, where are you? It's lunchtime." His mum's voice floated across the meadow.

"Quick, help me with this door," panted Oliver. Bertie heaved open the hay barn door and dived inside.

"Good, there's plenty of space. Hide over there in that corner. Well, as best you can, anyway. I have to go and have my lunch," Oliver explained to Bertie, "then I'll come back. Are you hungry?" he added.

Bertie nodded silently, afraid that if he spoke Oliver's mother might hear him. He couldn't stop his tummy rumbling though. It sounded just like thunder.

"I'll try and get you something to eat," Oliver promised and off he went, back to the house for lunch. He gobbled his lunch up as quickly as he could. He could hardly wait to get back to the barn and see his new

friend. As soon as he had finished eating he rushed back to Bertie.

He had brought Bertie a jam sandwich, which he'd hidden in his pocket. Bertie ate it in one bite. He was too polite to tell Oliver that giants make their sandwiches as big as double beds.

"Now," said Oliver, "we have to find my marble and a way to get you back home. You're too big to stay here and Dad said he had some work to do later in the barn — so we'd better hurry."

Bertie and Oliver crept out of the barn and back to the well. They both got down on their hands and knees and started searching for the marble. They searched and searched, but found nothing.

Eventually Bertie said, "I'm thirsty. Is there any water in your well?" He peered over the edge.

"No," said Oliver, "it's been filled in."

"Wait a minute," yelled the giant, causing the ground to shake and the trees to sway dangerously, "I think I've found it! There's something shining in the earth, about three feet down." He reached his long arm into the well, fished around a bit and brought out — the marble!

"Hooray! You've found it!" cried Oliver.

"Wow," gasped Bertie. "It's beautiful."

"Right, back to the barn," said Oliver excitedly. "It's time for some magic!"

Back in the barn Oliver and Bertie sat and rubbed their marbles and tried all the magic words they could think of, but the air didn't move, no 'whoomph' sound happened and Bertie stayed firmly in the barn with Oliver.

"Bertie," said Oliver, "would you like to swap marbles — like best friends do? We might even find a way to visit each other."

Bertie nodded, smiling enthusiastically. "I'd like you to visit me in the land of the giants," he said. In the distance Oliver could hear a tractor. "Oh no," he said. "I think my dad might be coming. We have to think of something, quickly! "

They rubbed the marbles harder and started to invent magic words and all the time the tractor was getting nearer. How would Oliver explain keeping a twelve-foot giant in the barn?

Then Bertie had an idea. "The air went 'whoomph' when I arrived, didn't it? So perhaps if we made the noise backwards it might magic me home."

Oliver and Bertie looked at each other.

"Bye," said Oliver, rubbing his eyes. "See you again?"

"Bye," said Bertie, sniffing. "I'll come back soon."

Oliver and Bertie rubbed their marbles hard, and together they said "Phmoohw." The air wobbled and shimmered a bit and in a flash Bertie was gone.

Outside the tractor noise stopped and a few seconds later Oliver's dad walked into the barn.

"Hello," he said. "What are you doing here? That's a pretty amazing marble," he added, nodding at Oliver's hand.

"Yes it is, isn't it?" Oliver held up the marble, which was as big as a doughnut, for his dad to see. "It's a giant-size one," he said, and smiled secretly to himself.

Bigger, Biggest, Best

Written by Dan Abnett

FORTYODD WAS A GIANT. He was called Fortyodd because he was forty-odd times as tall as a man. His hands were as big as bulldozers and his feet were as big as barges. He was huge. If you spread your arms out wide, it wouldn't be as wide as his smile.

Fortyodd was a gardener. He looked after the Great Forest. He strode through his forest in the way a farmer marches through his cabbage patch, bending over to prune an oak tree here, leaning down to replant a birch tree there.

Fortyodd liked his job. Fortyodd liked the Great Forest. He called it his lawn.

One morning, his friend Fifty-times came round and knocked on the door of his shed. Fortyodd's shed was nine times as large as an aircraft hangar, so the echo of Fiftytimes' knock rolled around the hills and dales for a week or two.

"Morning, Fiftytimes," rumbled

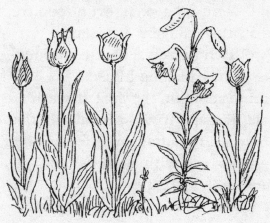

Fortyodd, as he came to the door of his shed, a steaming vat of tea in his hand. "The reservoir's just boiling. Do you fancy a vat of tea?"

"Don't mind if I do," replied Fiftytimes.

Fortyodd washed up another vat in his swimming pool-sized sink. He used a small evergreen tree as a brush. "Sugar?" he asked.

"Two barrows, please," replied Fiftytimes, making himself comfortable on the sofa. It wasn't a sofa, actually. It was a small hill that Fortyodd had dragged into the shed and covered with a circus tent, but they called it a sofa.

Fortyodd scooped two wheel-

barrows of sugar into Fiftytimes' vat
of tea and stirred it with a
lamppost.

"So what can I do for you?"
Fortyodd asked as they settled
down to their vats of tea.

"I thought I had better tell
you," said Fiftytimes, "old Twoscore
is planning to enter his prize
cabbage in the Harvest Show next
week. He's hoping to win the Big
Veg prize."

"I didn't know Twoscore had a
prize cabbage," said Fortyodd, rather
uneasily.

"That's why I thought I'd better
tell you," said Fiftytimes. "I was
passing his garden just yesterday,

and I saw his cabbage patch. It's a handsome crop he's got."

Fortyodd frowned. His brow crinkled so deeply, you could have lost whole flocks of sheep in the wrinkles. You see, every year, his famous pumpkins won the Big Veg rosette at the Harvest Show. There wasn't a giant in the land who grew vegetables that were bigger or better or more beautiful than Fortyodd's pumpkins.

"How are your pumpkins doing this year, anyway?" asked Fiftytimes.

Fortyodd took his friend out into the garden and showed him. There were a dozen splendid pumpkins, each one the size of a hot air balloon.

"Very impressive," said Fiftytimes, "but I have to say, old Twoscore's prize cabbage is bigger than your biggest pumpkin."

Fortyodd was very unhappy. After his friend had gone, he stomped about his garden, grumbling and moaning to himself. The ground shook, and from a mile away it sounded like a serious thunderstorm.

Fortyodd tried to do some weeding to take his mind off it, pulling up some chestnut trees, roots and all. But his heart wasn't in it. He went back to his shed and slammed the door behind him.

Fortyodd knew that he had to do something quickly, or Twoscore would win the prize. Fortyodd was very proud of the row of Big Veg rosettes over his fireplace, and couldn't bear the thought that there wouldn't be a new one to pin up this year. Besides, Big Veg was all he knew. It was his speciality. He hadn't got a particular talent for any of the other prize categories like jam making or tree. arranging.

Big Veg was his thing. He was a Big
Veg giant.

Fortyodd took down the
gardening book that his grandfather, old Seventysomething, had
compiled. It was chock full of
splendid tricks and tips. If nothing
else, old Seventysomething had
been the tallest gardener of his
generation.

Fortyodd laid the book open
on his desk. The open book was as
wide as the wingspan of a jumbo
jet.

Fortyodd put on his reading
glasses (two telescope lenses from
an observatory held in carefully
bent scaffolding) and studied the

book carefully, slowly turning the rugby pitch-sized pages.

Finally, just as it was getting dark, he found something.

There on page four thousand and one was a recipe for Plant Growth Formula. It seemed his grandfather had got the recipe from a retired witch.

That evening, Fortyodd made up the recipe. It took hours of careful mixing, measuring and stirring. At last, he was sure he had it pretty much right. He poured the formula out of the cement mixer and into a huge pair of furnace bellows. Then, with his lamp in one hand and the bellows in the other,

he went out into the dark, to his
pumpkin patch nearby. The
pumpkins looked huge and golden
in the moonlight.

Fortyodd took the bellows and
pumped a spray of formula over his
prize vegetables. The magic formula
twinkled electric green in the

darkness. Satisfied with a job well done, Fortyodd admired his handiwork. Already, the pumpkins looked even more huge and golden. Then Fortyodd went off to bed.

Next morning, Fortyodd's alarm (a church clocktower on the bedside table) woke him at eight, and he was surprised to see that it was still dark. He went to the door and tried to open it, but it wouldn't budge. He went to the window, and found he couldn't see anything outside except a wall of bright orange.

Rather worried, Fortyodd took the door off its hinges and found that the doorway was completely blocked by the biggest pumpkin he had ever seen. It was acres across from side to side. Fortyodd squeezed out of the doorway and climbed up onto the top of the enormous vegetable.

High up on top, it was like standing on an orange mountain, and there were several other orange mountains next to it. The huge pumpkins completely surrounded his garden shed, and seemed in danger of crushing it.

The formula had certainly worked.

Fortyodd wasn't really sure what to do next, but he knew that, one way or another, it would involve a lot of pumpkin-eating.

Everyone thereabouts agreed that Fortyodd's pumpkins were the biggest Big Veg they had ever seen. People flocked from miles around to see them. Families of giants had their photographs taken posing in front of the great pumpkin range. Passing dragons looked down at the pumpkins in astonishment. Dwarf mountaineers climbed them and stuck flags in the top.

Twoscore's prize cabbages won the Big Veg rosette at the Harvest Show, of course. Everyone said it was a shame. Fortyodd's pumpkins were the biggest in the world, but even with his friend Fiftytimes' help, he couldn't budge them an inch, let alone take them to the show! Still, he knew one thing — his grandfather would have been proud of him!

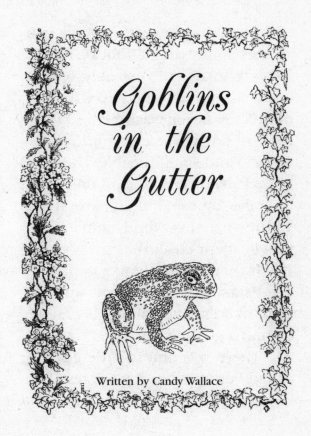

Goblins in the Gutter

Written by Candy Wallace

IF YOU'VE never met a goblin, you can count yourself lucky. They're very small and very ugly, with noses like needles and eyes like pins. They never wash behind their ears (or anywhere else, for that matter) and smell terrible. They live in dark, damp places, and only like to come out at night. But worst of all they hate everybody and every-thing-except custard.

If there's one thing a goblin can't stand it's a happy person. The sight of someone smiling is enough to ruin a goblin's week.

There was once a little girl called Poppy who was always happy. She had a nice mum and dad

and an older brother called Fred.
Now if you've got an older brother,
you probably think he's a pain in
the neck. But Poppy thought Fred
was the best thing since beef-
burgers.

"I'm really lucky to have a
brother like him," she would say to
her friends.

Poppy thought school was
absolutely brilliant, too. There was
nothing she liked more than two
pages of sums to do — unless it
was three pages of sums. Everybody
else thought Miss Crochet the
teacher was horrible and grumpy
and made them work too hard.
They put chewing gum on her

chair and daddy-long-legs in her
desk to make her screech. But
Poppy thought she was funny and
laughed at her.

Outside Poppy's house there
was a drain in the road. If you
looked down it all you could see
was dirty water at the bottom. It
was dark and smelly and full of old

lolly sticks, dead leaves and spiders.
There were goblins living in that
drain. You couldn't see them, but if
you knelt down and put your ear to
the ground you might have heard
them arguing. Goblins are always
arguing and fighting.

They had moved there when
Chestnut Tree Close was dug up to
lay new water pipes. They hadn't
minded the noisy road drills. But
laughing workmen who sang loud
songs and told jokes were more
than a goblin could stomach. So, at
dead of night, they had packed up
and made their way to Acacia
Avenue, and the drain outside
Poppy's house.

They soon realised this was a big mistake.

"It makes me feel sick," said Gruel, the oldest, grumpiest goblin, "every time I see Whatshername skipping along to school with a big smile on her face. She should be arrested for humming without due care and attention."

"Well, I think we should sort her out," said a fat goblin called Squelch, who thought all children should be made into savoury pies. "If we can't wipe that smile off her face, I'm a pixie."

The next morning, two goblins popped their heads through the grille of the drain. Their mean little eyes darted about to make sure no one was around. They jumped out holding a length of dirty old string, tied one end to the drain and tiptoed across the pavement to tie the other end to the hedge outside Poppy's house.

"There's nothing like a couple of grazed knees to make children cry!" sniggered one. "Let's hope she

enjoys the trip!" giggled the other and they jumped back inside the drain to wait and listen.

Sure enough, a few minutes later there was a cry and a commotion. Gleefully the goblins peeped out to survey their handiwork. But it wasn't Poppy they saw on the pavement — it was an old man, sitting with arms and legs waving in the air!

"Oh dear, oh dear!" said the old man. "Whatever happened? Thank goodness nothing's broken. I could have had a nasty fall!"

Poppy's mum and dad rushed out of the house to help him. So did Mr Entwhistle from across the road and Mrs Ramsbottom from number 67 .

"Are you all right, dear?" asked Poppy's mum, who was very worried about the old man. "Come on in and have a nice cup of tea. What horrid children would tie string across the path like that! Just wait till I catch them!"

"When you've had a nice cuppa I'll take you home," said Mrs Ramsbottom, anxiously.

"Thank you so much!" replied the old man, as they helped him out of the hedge. "Do you know, I've lived in this street for two years and no one has ever spoken to me before!" They all went into

Poppy's house. "Well you can come round for tea any time, Mr — er —."

"Brown. Ernest Brown," said the old man, and smiled to himself happily.

"Rats!" hissed Spodworthy, Goblin-in-Chief, to Gruel. "We got the wrong person! We'd better get it right next time! All we've done is make someone else happy too!"

That night, Squelch crept along the drains underground, up the pipes and through the plughole into the kitchen sink in Poppy's house. There on the table was her lunchbox for school, which Poppy's mum always packed the night before. He scurried to the rubbish

bin and picked out a horrible
smelly half-eaten fish. Then he
opened her lunch box, took out all
the cheese from the sandwiches

and put the fish in instead! He threw the cheese in the bin, and put the chocolate cake in his pocket for later!

"If that doesn't make her cry at school today, I don't know what will!" he smirked, and dived back down the plughole. Squelch couldn't think of anything worse than going without your lunch...

Poppy was none the wiser. In the morning she walked out of the garden gate holding her lunchbox and humming a tune.

Before long, she noticed a little cat following her, jumping up at the lunchbox and swiping it with her paw.

"Hello, pussycat!" said Poppy, bending down to stroke her. "Oh dear, you look very thin and your fur is all matted and dull. Haven't you got a home?"

The little cat gave a feeble miaow and sniffed and pawed at Poppy's lunchbox.

"You can have a sandwich if you like," said Poppy, and opened up her box. When she saw the fish sandwiches, she laughed. "Poor Mum must have been a bit muddled last night!" she said. "Come on, pussycat. Fred's always wanted a cat and you need someone to look after you."

Poppy picked up the cat and

took her home. Fred was thrilled. The goblins watched as Fred and Poppy fed the cat and played with her in the front garden. Spodworthy was beside himself with fury.

"Fools! Imbeciles! You've managed to turn one happy child and one miserable cat into two horribly happy children and one disgustingly happy cat!" he screamed at the other goblins.

That night, the goblins held a special committee meeting. They argued and shouted and jumped up and down. They boxed each others ears. Spodworthy stamped on Squelch's foot. Finally they came to a decision.

In the morning, Poppy kissed the cat (newly named Tiddles) goodbye and waved to Mr Brown. She skipped along the pavement, past the dark, silent drain.

The goblins had gone.

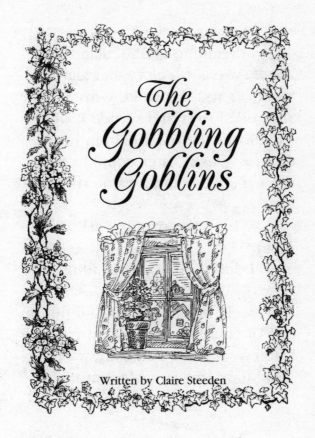

The Gobbling Goblins

Written by Claire Steeden

AMY WAS FAST ASLEEP and dreaming of chocolate cake. At eight o'clock her alarm went off and she woke with a start. She rolled over and turned it off. As she did so she felt a pain in her tummy. "Ouch. Mum, come here," she called. Her mum came running in.

"What's the matter?" asked her mum.

"I don't feel well. My tummy aches," said Amy.

"Well, stay in bed and I'll put on one of your story tapes and you can listen to it while I do some work," said Mum. Amy snuggled into her duvet listening to a story about

goblins, and gazing at the doll's
house in the corner of her room.
After a while she felt sleepy, but as
she began to doze she thought she
saw two little faces looking out
through her doll's house window.
She woke again later, when her
mum came into the room. "How are
you feeling?" asked Mum.

"I still feel a bit poorly. I just
had a funny dream about goblins
living in my doll's house," said Amy.

"There aren't any goblins in
your doll's house, silly," laughed
Mum.

"I wish there were. It would be
fun," said Amy.

"No it wouldn't. Goblins are

usually very naughty," said Mum. "Are you hungry? Would you like some lunch?"

"Not really," mumbled Amy.

"Well, how about a nice boiled egg with soldiers?" suggested Mum.

Amy followed her mum downstairs and lay on the sofa watching television while mum made lunch.

"Eat up," said Mum, as she set down a tray in front of Amy.

"But I don't feel very hungry," whined Amy.

"How about if I help you?" asked Mum, and she dipped the spoon into the egg. "O.K.," smiled Amy.

Just as the spoon got close to
Amy's mouth, the phone rang and
her mum turned away to answer it.
Amy was about to eat the egg when
two goblins ran out from behind
the salt and pepper pots, jumped
up and ate all the egg off the
spoon. Amy could not believe her
eyes! They looked just like the
goblins in her dream. They ran back
to their hiding place, giggling.

Amy's mum put the phone

down, turned back to Amy and looked at the spoon.

"So you are hungry after all," said Mum.

"I didn't eat it. It was the goblins hiding behind the pepper pot," said Amy, pointing to the tray. "Didn't you see them?"

"No," said Mum. "You and your goblins. Let's get on with lunch.

"But I'm not hungry," said Amy.

"Well, you soon gobbled the last spoonful. I know, if I look away

maybe the goblins will eat it again,"
laughed Mum. She was happy to
play Amy's game if it meant she ate
her lunch. So she dipped a soldier
into the egg, held it in front of Amy,
and looked away.

Amy sat and stared in
amazement as again the goblins
dashed out, ate the food and ran
back.

Amy started to giggle because
they looked so funny. Mum turned
back and saw that the soldier had
gone.

"Who could have eaten that?"
asked Mum with a smile.

"The goblins ate it," laughed
Amy.

"They must be hungry. Let's give them some more," said Mum. Amy and her mum sat on the sofa playing this game while the goblins ran back and forth eating Amy's lunch, until it was all gone. "That was fun," said Amy.

"Good," said Mum. "Lie here and watch television, and you'll soon start to feel better now you've eaten." As Mum left the room the goblins crept out and called to Amy. "Psstt, thanks for lunch."

"That's all right. I wasn't hungry. Where did you come from?" asked Amy.

"Oh, we live in a lovely little house upstairs," replied the goblins.

"What! In my doll's house? So it was your faces I saw at the window!" said Amy.

"Who are you talking to?" asked Mum, coming back into the room. "The goblins," answered Amy. "Look!" She pointed to where the goblins had been, but they had dived behind a cushion when they heard Mum coming.

"I think you've been dreaming again," said Mum.

Amy lay on the sofa watching T.V., but after a while she felt hungry, and asked her mum for something to eat.

"You can't feel hungry after eating all that lunch," said Mum

"But I didn't eat any lunch. The goblins did," whined Amy.

"Don't be silly. That was only a game."

"But they did eat it. They came downstairs from my doll's house," Amy explained.

"You've been having lots of funny dreams this morning while you've been poorly. There are no such things as goblins," laughed Mum.

"There are. They're real. I saw them. And they ate my lunch and now I'm hungry," said Amy.

Munch whispered something to Crunch and they jumped down onto the floor and dashed into the doll's house. Amy sat and waited, but not for long. Soon Munch and Crunch came running out with trays filled with all the plastic food from the doll's house kitchen. "I can't eat that," laughed Amy, "it's not real."

"Of course you can eat it," said Munch. "Watch."

With that Munch and Crunch held hands and started jumping up and down.

As they did so they called out,

"Plastic food, you look so yummy.

Become real, to fill my tummy!"

With that there was a bright flash, and when Amy opened her

eyes there in front of her was a real feast! "Oh, wow," she cried. "Thank you."

Amy tucked into sandwiches, cakes, crisps, sausage rolls, biscuits and ice cream.

After a while she said, "I'm full. I can't eat any more. Thank you."

"We'd better clear up before your mum comes," said Crunch. With another flash all the food vanished.

"We'd better go. Sorry you got into trouble, but I hope you enjoyed our lunch," said Crunch.

"Oh, I did. It was much nicer than a boiled egg," said Amy and they all laughed. They said goodbye and in a flash the goblins had gone.

Amy was just licking the last bit of ice cream from her lips when Mum came in with a tray of food.

"I thought that you might want some tea and biscuits," said Mum.

"Yes, please," said Amy.

Mum sat on the bed and gave Amy the tray. Just then the phone rang and Mum went to answer it. When she came back all the biscuits had gone.

"Who ate all those?" asked Mum.

"I did," replied Amy. "The goblins have gone home."

A Nasty Case of Goblins

Written by Dan Abnett

LORD DUBLOON of Steep Castle took a step back in amazement. "I've g...got wh..what?" he stammered.

The dwarf from the Council straightened the front of his overalls and tucked his stubby pencil behind his stubby ear. "You've got the worst case of goblins I've seen in all my long years."

Lord Dubloon's legs suddenly decided he needed to sit down, and he staggered backwards onto his huge chair. "Goblins?" he asked. "In my castle?"

The dwarf nodded and shrugged. "No doubt about it, your

Lordship. You have got what we in
the pest control business call an
infestation. They're everywhere."

Lord Dubloon sagged. "This is
terrible. The neighbours will talk.
I'm a respectable lord, I've got
responsibilities. I have to wear a
robe and medals and give orders
and have banquets and ... and
things. I can't have the family castle
overrun with goblins." He said the
word like it was the rudest one
he'd ever heard.

He got to his feet. "Are you
quite sure?" he asked, hoping it was
all a joke.

The dwarf nodded, pointing to
a stretch of skirting board between

two suits of armour. "Look," he said. "That hole. .."

"Mice!" said Lord Dubloon quickly.

"Mice don't need a hole a foot high, your Lordship," said the dwarf. "Listen..." He knelt down and rapped hard on the wooden skirting. Lord Dubloon leaned over to hear.

The unmistakable sound of cackling laughter floated up out of the hole. Goblins, sniggering.

The dwarf looked up at Lord Dubloon. "Goblins," he stated, somewhat shortly.

Lord Dubloon sighed and thought for a while. "Can you do anything about them?" he asked.

The dwarf frowned and whistled through his teeth. "No," he said, at last. "But," he added, "I know a dwarf who can."

A second dwarf arrived at Steep Castle the next morning, pushing a handcart with a sign painted on the side. The sign read:

"Short Brothers, Pest Control. Biggest in the business. Gorgons, Goblins and Cockroaches a speciality." Lord Dubloon hurried outside. "Lord Dubloon! A pleasure!" said Mr Short smartly. "They tell me it's goblins you've got."

Lord Dubloon nodded.

"Right ho!" said the dwarf. He

put on a pair of big leather gloves, a
pair of rubber waders, a welding
mask and goggles, and a hard hat
with a miner's lamp attached to it.

"Mmmgg mghhmmp ggmmgp
hhgg," he said.

"Pardon?" asked Lord Dubloon.

Mr Short raised the visor of his
welding mask. "Show me the way!"
he repeated. "And could you give
me a hand with my equipment?"

Weighed down with ropes and
ladders and sink plungers and
butterfly nets, Lord Dubloon led Mr
Short into the Grand Hall.

The dwarf dropped onto his
hands and knees and crawled over
to the hole in the skirting board. He

tapped at the wood. They heard goblin laughter.

"Down to business," said Mr Short.

Later that morning, Lord Dubloon returned to the Grand Hall to see how things were going. Mr Short had certainly been busy . All the furniture had been pushed back and covered with dust sheets, and scaffolding had been erected along the wall over the hole in the skirting board.

Pulleys and ropes held a huge net across the roof, and other ropes ran down to the floor, where they were trapped under a large cast iron tub. The tub itself was perched on the end of a plank of wood that was balanced on a barrel like a see-saw.

High above, Lord Dubloon's chair dangled from the scaffolding on a rope. In another corner of the room was a rack of fireworks. Mr Short sat under the scaffolding, slowly fitting together a long, flexible pole.

Lord Dubloon edged across to the tub perched on the see-saw and looked in. It was full of custard.

"Careful there, your Lordship. Custard. Very precarious. This whole apparatus is on a hair trigger."

"What is all this?" asked Lord Dubloon.

"Short's Patent Goblin Trap," replied Mr Short, proudly. "Allow me to explain. They love custard, do goblins, can't get enough of it. They come out of their hole to get to the custard. I light the fireworks. Boom! Bang! Whizz! Very pretty. Goblins love fireworks too. So they're all stood round the custard tub, and they're looking up admiring the fireworks. But ... one of the fireworks is aimed at the rope holding the throne. It cuts through it. The throne drops onto the see-saw, the tub flies into the air, covering the goblins in sticky custard. They can't move, and the net floats down and traps them. Bingo!"

Lord Dubloon nodded, uncertainly. "So why do they come out of the hole in the first place?" he asked. Mr Short held up the long, flexible pole. On the end was a sign that said:

"HEY! GOBLINS! CUSTARD! THIS WAY!"

"This will fetch them out," said Mr Short. "Now, would you be so kind as to poke this pole down the hole?"

Lord Dubloon did so, as Mr Short stood by the fireworks with a lighted match. Lord Dubloon suddenly felt the pole being tugged out of his hands. It disappeared into the hole Hearing excited goblin voices, he backed away. A moment later, a dozen little, green, pointy-eared, fanged, wicked, giggling goblins came rushing out of the skirting board, and headed straight for the custard.

"Bingo!" cried Short, and lit the fireworks. They went off with a bang. It all happened very quickly. The goblins went "Oooohhh!" as they looked up at the fireworks shooting madly around the hall. Then they picked up the tub and ran for the hole in the skirting board.

One firework released the chair, which crashed down and shattered, pinging the see-saw through a window with a loud crash.

The net was already falling. Mr Short, who was being chased by a firework, caught his foot in a stray rope and disappeared up to the ceiling, where he dangled upside down.

Lord Dubloon looked at the devastation that had been his Grand Hall.

He wanted to sit down, but his chair had been smashed into firewood.

Just then, the flexible pole poked back out of the goblin hole with a very badly written note on the end of it.

It read: "tHAnkS FoRe ThE cusTaRd. yor Klown wAs vERy FUnny. mAkE him do It AgAiN."

Fuming, Lord Dubloon looked up at Mr Short. "Bingo?"

"Just a temporary setback, your Lordship," began Mr Short. "Er. . . do you think you could help me down from here?"

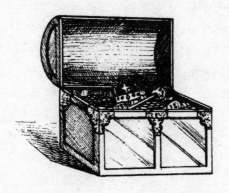

Lord Dubloon winced as the echoes of goblin laughter floated out from the skirting board. "I'll make 'short' work of you when I do!"

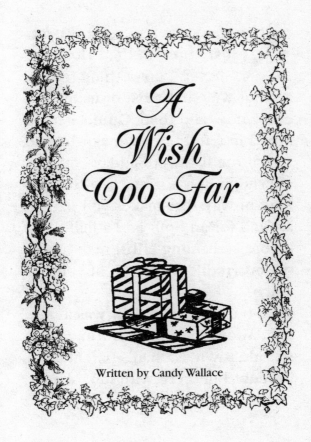

A Wish Too Far

Written by Candy Wallace

NATHAN WAS BORED. He wasn't just bored in that "Ho Hum! I haven't got a thing to do!" kind of way that most of us feel every now and then. Oh no, he was bored in a full blown, major league, top of the list, wet Sunday afternoon in a boring seaside town kind of way, that makes you pace around for an hour and a half before screaming, "IIIIII'm boooorrred!!" at the top of your voice.

Strangely enough, it was a wet Sunday afternoon in a boring seaside town. Nathan's parents had brought him here with talk of a "lovely week in a delightful town by the sea". So far, the "lovely" and "delightful" parts of his parents' description had most definitely failed to appear.

Certainly, they had spent the better part of a week in a town by the sea (which was a distinctly murky shade of grey, by the way), but "lovely" and "delightful"? No, these weren't the words that sprang into Nathan's mind. It had, after all, rained for half the time and poured with rain for the other half.

The gloomy atmosphere that hung over the town was like the feeling you get when you're waiting for a kiss from a particularly ugly, long lost aunt!

Making matters worse was the fact that his little sister, Janine, and his little brother, Christian, were having a lovely time playing happily together. The miserable weather didn't seem to bother them. They were just as happy to play indoors.

Nathan just wanted the holiday to be over and to get back home. Unfortunately, they still had another two days to go.

Nathan paced up and down, sat grumpily in a chair (ignoring the book that his dad had bought for him), or sat in front of the television, flicking between the channels. And still the rain pitter-pattered against the window.

"I wish I could be on my own somewhere, without my family getting under my feet!" he thought, gloomily.

Finally, he got up and grabbed his coat. "Where are you going?" asked his mum.

"Into the garden!" he replied.

His mum sighed wearily. "But it's still raining!"

Nathan put on his coat.

"I don't care!" he said. "I'm going to stand in the garden and grow roots and become a tree and then I'll be stuck here for ever!" And with that, he stomped out.

"Cor!" said Janine, excitedly. "That sounds brilliant! Come on, Chris, let's go and watch!"

Out in the garden, Nathan splashed across the muddy grass with his sister and brother following closely behind. As they neared the far end of the garden, Nathan turned to the others and began to snarl at them, continuing to walk backwards as he did so.

"Why don't you leave me alone?" he snapped.

"We want to see you turn into a tree!" Christian replied.

"Ohhh… that's all I need…" Nathan began, but was cut off as he disappeared from sight. Janine and Christian stopped in their tracks.

They looked down and saw a hole in the ground where Nathan

had been walking. Peering down into it, they jumped back with shock as Nathan's head popped up.

"Aaaaahhhh!" they screamed in unison.

"It's okay!" replied Nathan. "The hole wasn't very deep! And look what I found down there…"

Nathan held up a small, shiny box that gleamed and sparkled, even in the gloomy rain.

"What is it?" Janine asked.

Just as she spoke, the box slipped from Nathan's fingers and landed on the wet grass. The lid flipped open and a twinkly swirl of light flew into the air. The children gasped in amazement, as a tiny figure materialised in front of them. A man, no more than five or six inches tall, hovered in the air before landing on a nearby sunflower. He had a bushy white beard and was wearing a pointed red hat.

"Ohhhh…" he groaned. "My

aching back! I've been in that box for bloomin' years!"

Nathan, eyes and mouth wide with surprise, asked the little man who and what he was.

"I'm Eric!" he stated, puffing out his chest proudly. "Eric the Elf, young sir! You have freed me from a trap set for me a long time ago by a particularly grumpy wizard!"

"You're an elf?!" Nathan said. "That's incredible!"

The little elf looked flattered.

"You said it, young man!" he replied. "I am incredible. And seeing as how you've freed me from that box, and furthermore, seeing as how you seem to be a young man of exceedingly good taste, I will grant you three wishes!"

Barely pausing for thought, Nathan said, "I wish my family would disappear!" With a tinkling of bells, Janine, Christian and their parents promptly vanished. Nathan sat on the wet grass, not quite believing what had happened.

"Is… is that it?" he asked. "Are they r…really gone?"

Eric gestured around the garden. "Look around you !" he said. Certainly, Janine and Christian were no longer there. Eric leant forwards and prodded Nathan. "Listen, sonny, I'm a busy elf! What's your second wish?"

"I wish I was somewhere nice and hot, all by myself!" Nathan answered. And suddenly, he was alone on a beautiful beach, the blue sky arching high over his head and the sea glittering like polished diamonds and stretching away for ever.

"Wow!" Nathan said, getting to his feet and running across the hot sand. "This is brilliant, eh, Eric? Eric?" There was no answer. Nathan whirled around quickly, looking everywhere. "Eric?" he shouted again, but there was no reply, only the sound of the sea, lapping gently at the shore.

He ran around for what seemed

like ages, but the empty beach seemed to have no end, and the tropical forest that bordered the beach looked a bit dark and scary.

Finally, hot, tired and more than a little worried, he flopped down on the sand and began to sob quietly. If only he could be back with all his family around him in that funny little bungalow on the edge of the wet and dreary seaside town!

"Well, I'm sure that can be arranged!" said a little voice at Nathan's side, making him jump. It was Eric. "You said you wanted to be alone, so I thought I'd give you a little time to yourself!"

"I want to go back and I want my family to be back with me!" Nathan said, breathlessly.

"And is that your third and final wish, then?" Eric asked. Nathan nodded his head vigorously.

"Oh, it is! It is!" he said.

"I'll see what I can do," said Eric.

Janine tugged at his arm and

Nathan felt the rain against his face. "Come up out of that hole!" she said, as she and Christian peered down at him. Nathan climbed out of the damp hole and looked around, feeling very glad to be back. He could see his mum and dad inside the house and thought to himself that it was one of the nicest sights he had ever seen.

"Your brother and sister won't remember me!" Eric said, appearing in front of Nathan. "But I think you will, and you'll remember what you learnt today!"

"You bet!" Nathan said. "I'll never take my family for granted again! Even if they do bring me for a lovely week in a delightful town by the sea!"

And as Eric twinkled from sight, Nathan looked up at the grey sky, took his sister's hand, and ran inside laughing to join his family!

Puffcheek's Palace

Written by Geoff Cowan

IF YOU WALK carefully and quietly through a woodland dell, don't be startled to hear faint voices and glimpse some colourfully dressed little people. For there may be elves and pixies about, just like there were in the woods behind the garden of Kate's cottage home. Only, her brother Sam didn't believe her. Then something very strange happened that made him begin to wonder…

"Pull!" cried Topknot, sitting grandly on a small carriage he had found while going early-morning exploring.

He had fetched the other elves, and they were using a rope of woven grass to tow his discovery away. However, nothing much happened in those woods without the sharp-eyed pixies noticing. When they saw the carriage, they wanted to join in the fun.

"Push!" shouted Puffcheek to his fellow pixies.

So the elves pulled the carriage while the pixies pushed, until it lurched and Topknot almost fell off.

"Pulling's safer than pushing me along!" he called, grumpily.

"But pushing's easier, especially if you go downhill!" protested Puffcheek. "Watch! We'll show you!"

Before Topknot could stop them, Puffcheek and the other

STORIES FOR THE YOUNG READER

pixies gave such a mighty shove
that the carriage suddenly sped
forward. It moved so fast that the
startled elves hardly had time to
jump out of the way.

Now, Topknot did topple off.
He landed safely and softly on the
thick grass while the carriage
hurtled into a deep ditch and
overturned, its wheels spinning in
the air.

"That was your fault,
Puffcheek!" snapped Topknot. "When
it comes to being useful, pixies
should learn a lesson from elves!"

Suddenly, heavy footsteps saved
an argument as they all raced for
cover.

"There it is!" cried Kate, pointing. "What a place to leave your skateboard!"

"I didn't!" replied Sam. "I told you! I put it down by a tree at the edge of the woods while I collected some conkers that had fallen. I couldn't carry everything home in one go. Then Mum called us for tea and I forgot all about my skateboard until today. Someone must have moved it!"

"Pixies and elves, I suppose!" smiled Kate.

Sam laughed and scrambled into the ditch. He picked up his skateboard, then headed for home. Kate was about to follow when she spotted the elves' grass rope that had broken free from the skateboard. Kate looked at it thoughtfully and put it in her pocket.

"So that's where the carriage came from," said Topknot, afterwards.

"You mean skateboard," corrected Puffcheek. "The Big People use all kinds of odd things and give them some very funny names!"

"Well, whatever they call it, I want it back!" cried Topknot. "Finders keepers. That's only fair!"

Even the pixies agreed, so Puffcheek had no choice but to try and recover the skateboard.

Which brought him to Kate's

cottage garden. Sam had already gone to meet a friend, taking the skateboard with him. Meanwhile, Kate sat at the far end of the garden to examine the little grass rope. Puffcheek crept closer, searching for the skateboard. Suddenly, Kate sneezed and blew the pixie off a log he had clambered on to.

"Hey! Look out, clumsy!" he yelled and Kate was just close enough to hear.

"Oh, there really are pixies," she cried. "Did you make this rope?"

"No, it was the elves!" replied Puffcheek, picking himself up.

Then he remembered how

much larger Big People were and was about to hurry away. It was only the thought of facing an angry Topknot without the skateboard that stopped him.

"I'll weave you a grass bracelet if you give me that carriage, er, skateboard," said Puffcheek.

"I was right! You did move it!" said Kate. "But the skateboard's not mine!"

Puffcheek explained what had happened. Then he sighed, "I can't return empty-handed to Topknot!"

Kate remembered something and had an idea. "Come back as the sun goes down and I may be able to help. "

Unbeknown to Kate, Sam had arrived home and come into the garden.

"Who were you talking to?" he asked Kate, puzzled.

"Oh, just a pixie!" she replied, playfully. "You know you tidied up your cupboard yesterday. Didn't you say you wanted to get rid of your toy castle?" Kate asked.

Sam nodded. "I'm too big for it now!"

"I know someone who's just the right size!" said Kate. "Can I have it?"

"If you like," said Sam.

When Sam went inside, Kate fetched the little castle, complete with its turrets, drawbridge and battlements. She took it to the edge of the wood. At dusk, Puffcheek found the castle with a note from Kate telling him it was for Topknot.

"I'm sorry I was cross with you, Puffcheek!" said Topknot as, this time, the elves and pixies happily pushed and pulled the toy castle deeper into the woods. "A castle's better than a carriage any day!"

"You can call it 'Topknot's Castle'," said Puffcheek.

"Or 'Puffcheek's Palace'," replied Topknot kindly. "It's yours as long as we can play inside and have parties there! After all, you were very brave to speak to one of the Big People!"

Puffcheek smiled proudly as the elves and pixies congratulated him.

Next morning, before school, Sam followed his sister into the garden.

"I saw you carrying my castle

down to the bottom of the garden last night," he said. "You wanted to play with it yourself all along, didn't you?"

"No, I left it here," replied Kate, pointing. "But it's gone!"

"Just like my skateboard," said Sam, thoughtfully. "Shall we search for it?"

"No," replied Kate, who was very pleased to have helped Puffcheek and the others.

"Don't tell me you think the elves and pixies took my old toy castle too!" grinned Sam.

Kate nodded. "Who else?" she smiled. "Only, this time, I think we'll let them keep it!"

Playful the Pixie

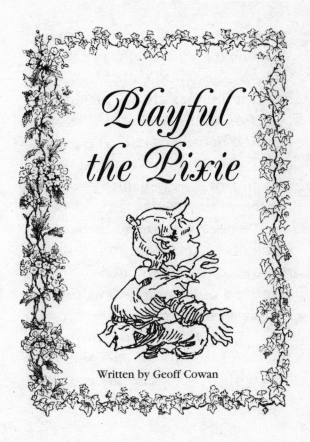

Written by Geoff Cowan

PLAYFUL lived up to his name. That's what the other pixies in the wood called him because he was always playing tricks on them. At first they laughed because pixies do get up to mischief once in a while. But Playful's pranks began to get out of hand.

"Wheee!" he yelled as he suddenly swung on a strand of ivy right towards Picklepot, who was sipping a cup of cold dewdrop tea. It spilt all over him.

"Ooh! Ow!" yelled Sunnysmile, as Playful lay in wait and pelted him with berries. The juice stained Sunnysmile's clothes.

"Grrrgh!" spluttered an unsus-
pecting Curlytoes when he pulled
on his hat and found Playful had
filled it with water. Truth was, the
pixies were more than a little tired
of Playful's non-stop naughtiness.
Time and again they asked him to
behave.

"A joke's a joke but you've
gone too far, Playful," they warned.

"Or not far enough!" grumbled
some. "Keep this up and you can go
and play in someone else's patch of
wood!"

Which is exactly what Playful
did. One morning, he climbed out
of bed extra early and set off
across the meadow into another

wood where a band of elves lived. And what a dance he led them, too. Playful made sure he kept himself hidden and puffed pollen on the elves to make them sneeze. While they slept, he swapped their boots around so they didn't fit!

"This is better fun than before," giggled Playful. "Now no one even knows it's me!"

That was until the elves caught him, for elves are much more clever than you might think. They knew someone had to be behind all the odd goings-on, so they laid a trap.

Playful fell for it; or it fell for Playful, to be exact. A carefully placed bag of honey dropped on his hat, bursting open, the next time he tried to creep up on the elves.

"Caught you!" they cried, feeling extremely pleased with themselves as they danced around a very gooey Playful.

"Mess with us and you'll come unstuck!" warned an elf named Echo. He was called Echo because he liked the sound of his own voice.

"I'm in a mess and all stuck up!" cried Playful, miserably.

"Serves you right!" sang Echo. "When you're washed and clean, we'll take you back where you came from."

One of the elves had guessed Playful was from The Other Wood because he'd heard it was full of pixies. When both bands came face to face, the pixies were startled to see Playful with the elves. They weren't so surprised to hear about all the bother he'd caused.

"The least we can do is invite you to a Pixie Party," Picklepot told the elves. "There'll be music, dancing and all the pixie pizzas you can eat!"

And more of Playful's pranks. The fact was he just couldn't seem to help himself. He sprinkled mud on the mushroom seats to make folk sit down with a squelch! He put jelly in a flower-trumpet so wobbly bits were blown out everywhere when the pixie band played; and that was only the start.

The elves and pixies were fed up before they'd even eaten anything! When they did sit down to eat they were furious to discover that someone had mixed up all the food and put mustard in the jam sandwiches and tomato ketchup in the sponge cake. Things had gone beyond a joke!

It called for quick thinking before tempers flared. Picklepot and Echo drew up a plan. The first part was easy. For the rest of the party, the elves and pixies would take it in turns to watch Playful very carefully. If he showed the slightest sign of mischief, they would step in and stop him. The second part was harder…

Next morning, when Playful woke, what do you think his first thought of the day was? Which new tricks he should try out, of course! But he never got the chance to play any tricks, because he realised with a terrible shock that he had no idea where he was.

And even worse, he was all alone.
He was in a part of the wood he
had never been to before.

"Trembling toadstools! Where
am I?" gasped Playful, sitting up
with a start. "Where is everyone?"

Before Playful could throw
back his patchwork blanket, it flew
off as if by magic, leaving him lying
in his night-shirt.

"What's happening?" gasped
Playful, reaching for the folded
green tunic on the end of the bed.
He went to pull it on and found he
couldn't. It was much too tiny!

"Hey! That's not mine!" he
cried, crossly.

At least the boots fitted but

these weren't his either and they
had big holes in the soles. Next
moment, Playful spotted a folded
piece of paper on the ground. His
name was written on it in large

letters. As Playful hurried to pick it up, the paper danced into the air then settled close by.

Playful hoped there might be a map on the other side to show him the way home. But every time he neared the paper, it fluttered further away until it landed long

enough to Playful to pounce. Whoosh! A net hidden under some leaves sprang up and closed around him. Playful was whisked off his feet and found himself dangling in mid-air.

"Caught you!" cried a voice as Playful struggled.

"Let me down, whoever you are! Please stop playing tricks on me!" he called, dizzily. He was really rather frightened indeed.

"Only if you stop playing them on all of us!" said Picklepot, who stepped out from behind a tree with the other pixies.

"And us! And us!" repeated Echo who appeared with the elves.

"Yes! I promise!" said Playful, who was relieved to see them. They gently lowered the net and helped him out.

Now Playful noticed Sunnysmile holding the bed blanket tied to a long thread that he had used to pull it away. Another was tied to the note Playful had chased to lure him to the net. Curlytoes happily handed over Playful's proper clothes.

"We carried your bed here while you slept," grinned Picklepot. "Then we set up the other tricks."

"They're not funny when someone plays them on you, are they?" said Echo sternly.

"I hadn't thought of that," agreed Playful, shaking his head. "It isn't very nice, is it? I promise that from today I won't play any more tricks on anyone. Except maybe just a small one on Sundays."

The elves and the pixies all chuckled, and Picklepot said that was good enough for him. The elves agreed and returned to their own wood. From that day on, Playful was the best-behaved pixie you could imagine — except on Sundays, when everyone wondered who's turn it would be for him to play tricks on!

The pixies even gave him a new name 'Goodasgold', and he

became a very helpful little pixie indeed.

So if you ever chance to meet a very polite pixie, remember who it could be and be careful never to ask him, "How's tricks?!"

Especially on a Sunday!

Trading Places

Written by Amber Hunt

KATINA HATED being a pixie.
Her parents said it was a
pixie's job to look after the
woodland they lived in, but Katina
thought that was boring. What she
really wanted to be was a Tooth
Fairy and to dress in beautiful fairy
clothes and carry a wand, some
fairy dust, and the special Tooth
Fairy bag. But Katina was a pixie, so
she wiped the dew off the grass
and polished the leaves and painted
and scented the flowers and all the
time she was fed up, bored and
grumpy.

In fact, Katina was so grumpy
that all her friends had started
flying away when they saw her. So

now Katina was not only fed up, bored and grumpy, but also lonely too.

Then, early one sunny morning, when Katina was naughtily painting a flower a particularly nasty shade of yucky purple and scenting it with a really horrible smell, she thought she heard someone crying.

Katina stopped and listened. There it was again, someone was definitely crying.

"Well, tough," she thought. "Nobody cares that I'm miserable, so why should I care just because someone is crying," and she went back to what she was doing.

But the crying didn't stop and eventually Katina's curiosity got the better of her and she went to have a look.

It was coming from a clump of bluebells. Well, they would have been blue if Katina hadn't painted them a sickly green yellow. They should have smelled nice too, but they didn't.

Katina tip-toed up to the smelly clump of greeny-yellow bells and peeped through.

There behind them was … a Tooth Fairy!

"Gosh," said Katina. "A Tooth Fairy! Why are you crying?"

"Because I'm upset, stupid," snapped the Tooth Fairy.

"Oh well, fine," said Katina, "if that's how you feel, you can jolly well go on crying," and she went to fly off.

"No wait," said the fairy. "I'm sorry, I'm not usually rude. It's just that I've sprained my wing and I can't fly." Turning round she showed Katina her hurt wing.

"Oh," said Katina. "What are you going to do?"

"I don't know," sniffed the fairy. "I'm supposed to be visiting a little girl and we never let children down. But there's only a short time left before the little girl wakes up. She'll be so disappointed if her tooth is still there and there's no coin." The fairy started crying again.

"Oh, for goodness sake," said Katina. "Do stop. I'll take you to see my mum and dad. I expect they'll know what to do."

Katina helped the fairy out of the greeny-yellow bells. "What's that horrid smell?" asked the fairy. "And why are those flowers such a revolting colour?"

"Oh, a naughty pixie did that," explained Katina.

"Dreadful," said the fairy. "I hope you don't do things like that." She gave Katina a long hard stare .

As they walked along, Katina suddenly stopped in her tracks. "I've got an idea," she gasped, amazed at her own daring. "I can

fly, so why don't I take the coin to the little girl for you and bring you back her tooth? Please let me," she begged.

The fairy looked at Katina thoughtfully, "All right," she said eventually. "There isn't much time though, and you must do exactly as I say." She gave Katina precise instructions and made Katina repeat them back to her three times before she was satisfied. Finally, she gave Katina the special Tooth Fairy bag and sent her on her way.

Katina flew through the woodland bursting with joy. If she did this well, perhaps she would be

allowed to become a Tooth Fairy
one day.

The Tooth Fairy sat and waited,
feeling rather worried. Then, as the
sun was rising further in the sky
and it was approaching the time
when humans wake up, Katina
returned. She flew to the fairy's
side and collapsed in a panting,
dirty and rather smelly heap.

"I did it," she gasped, holding
out the bag to the fairy, and then
added, "Is it always like that?"

"Like what, exactly?" asked the
fairy.

"Well," said Katina, "I flew out
of the woodland and in the
direction you said, when suddenly

there was a terrible noise and this huge horrible monster came screaming right at me. I flew for my life and barely escaped."

The fairy nodded knowingly and said, "I think you will find that was one of the cars I warned you about. They are very dangerous, but they never leave the road the humans built for them to run on."

"Oh," said Katina, impressed by the fairy's knowledge. "Then I was chased by a big hairy monster with enormous eyes, massive fangs and hot evil smelling breath."

The fairy laughed.

"That was a dog. They are friendly and mostly they just want to play, but you have to be careful that you don't accidentally get squashed by them."

"After that," went on Katina, "I was chased by another, smaller monster. This one had big green eyes, sharp teeth and claws and it hissed at me. I had to hide in a smelly hill near the little girl's house, until it went away."

"Ah," sighed the fairy, "that was a cat. You have to be careful with cats. Sometimes they just want to play, but sometimes they can be very spiteful. You were wise to hide, although I suspect that what you hid in was called a compost heap. You really do smell quite unpleasant you know."

"Thanks a lot," sniffed Katina.

"You know," the Tooth Fairy went on, "since you've done so well the Grand Fairy Committee might consider allowing you to attend the Tooth Fairy School."

Katina smiled. "No thank you," she said. "I thought I wanted to be a Tooth Fairy, but after today, I've

decided I'm very happy being a
pixie.

"And no more nasty coloured
flowers with horrible smells?"
asked the fairy.

"Ah," said Katina, "you knew.
No," she promised, "and I won't be
grumpy any more either."

The fairy nodded, pleased, and
gave Katina a big hug. Then, arm in
arm, they went off through the
woodland. The Tooth Fairy's wing

soon recovered and she became the best of friends with Katina, who kept her little patch of woodland spotless.

Magic Mix-up

Written by Claire Steeden

ONE SUNNY MORNING Wanda the Witch woke up, rubbed her eyes and climbed out of her rather saggy bed. She put on her favourite black dress with purple stars. It was quite tatty as she wore it every day. She tied a belt round her plump belly and pulled on her shoes with curly wurly toes. Then she pushed her hair up into her pointy hat as it was so tangled she could not get a brush through it. She looked in the mirror and laughed.

"What a mess. Still, I've no time to waste on myself."

Wanda was always busy doing spells for her friends. Her 'rock into enormous sticky chocolate pudding' spell was frequently in demand. However, her wand had never been quite the same since it had fallen into her cauldron and her spells often got in a muddle.

This morning Wanda had an important spell to do. Harriet the Hedgehog was having a birthday party for her son Harry that afternoon, and Wanda was making a special cake. She lifted her enormous book of spells off the shelf, popped her glasses on her long nose and peered at the first page.

"Bestest birthday cakes," she read out, "page seventy-three."

She turned the pages filled
with magic. "Let's see what we
need. One large frog, got that, a cup
of rats' tails, got that, some slimy
slugs, got them, and a pretty,
scented flower for decoration.
Bother, I haven't got one of those.
Mix together, throw mixture into
the air, wave your wand and say the
magic words:

'Up in the air, twist and shake,
Make me the bestest birthday
cake.'

Well that sounds simple. I just need to go and pick a flower." Wanda put on her shawl and bustled down the garden path and into the forest, where she found a small bush with the prettiest flowers. Wanda bent down to pick one, held it under her nose to sniff and tucked it into her pocket.

As she stood up she heard someone humming close by. Wanda crept behind a huge oak tree. Peeping out, she saw the beautiful Princess Primula, who had long golden curly hair, big brown eyes, dainty little hands and a gorgeous sparkly pink gown. Wanda looked down at herself and realised how shabby and ugly she was. At that moment Princess Primula rounded the tree and came face to face with Wanda. The princess let out an almighty scream and ran away as fast as she could.

"I must have really scared her. She is so beautiful and I'm so ugly." A tear rolled down Wanda's cheek. Then she had an idea. "I'm always doing magic for other people. I should do some for myself. I'll go home and make myself as beautiful as the princess."

Picking up her skirt she ran as fast as her short fat legs could carry her. Wanda flicked through her book of spells and found a spell to

make lovely long hair. She took off
her hat, picked up her wand and
said the magic words:

"*Take away this tangled mess,*
  and in its place put hair.
As long and fine as it can be,
  to make me look most fair."

But when she felt her head,
instead of soft silky hair, she felt
something smooth and shiny. She
was completely bald!

"Oh bother," she cried. "This stupid wand. I'll have to buy a new one the next time I go to Witchways. Oh well, I'll come back to my hair later. I think I'll try making my hands and feet smaller."

Wanda found the right spell and read it out carefully.

"My hands and feet are far too big,
I'd like them to be tiny.
With skin as soft as purest silk,
And nails all long and shiny."

But, oh dear, when Wanda held out her arms there at the end were two dainty little feet.

When she stuck out her legs there were two pretty hands on the end of each. "Drat and blast. What a muddle. Oh well, I'll sort them out later."

Wanda decided to try to make her nose and chin less pointed.

She read out the spell:

"Go away you pointy nose,
and you pointy chin.
Instead be nice and rounded,
pretty, small and trim."

She waved her wand above her head and hoped the spell had worked. But, oh dear, guess what happened. A very pretty little nose appeared, but not where a nose should be. It was on her chin, which was now much smaller.

"I'm really getting in a muddle. I'll try one more time, then I'd better sort out all those mixed-up spells. I think I'll try a spell to make me thinner."

"Bulges on my belly,
bulges on my thighs.
Go away and don't come back,
please be a smaller size."

With a wave of her wand she was instantly so thin that her dress

fell off her shoulders and onto the floor. Wanda was left standing in the kitchen in just her underwear!

At that moment Harriet the Hedgehog knocked at the door and came in. She took one look at Wanda and burst into a fit of giggles. "What on earth are you doing?"

"I was trying to make myself beautiful," replied Wanda.

"Well, it looks like things have gone a bit wrong. Go and look at yourself in the mirror," giggled Harriet.

Wanda stood in front of her mirror and started to laugh.

"Oh dear, this really isn't quite

what I had in mind. What a muddle," said Wanda.

"Why do you want to look beautiful?" asked Harriet. Wanda explained what had happened in the forest.

"Well, I don't know why you're making such a fuss. Although Princess Primula is beautiful on the outside, she's horrible inside. She's mean and selfish and nobody likes her," explained Harriet. "You may not be beautiful but you are kind and helpful and everybody loves you."

Wanda thought about this. "Yes, I do have lots of friends and that is more important than being beautiful. I'd better get out of this muddle and get on with Harry's cake."

Wanda cancelled all the spells, put her dress back on and turned to the birthday cake spell. She mixed the ingredients in her cauldron, threw the mixture in the air, and said the magic words:

"Up in the air, twist and shake.
Make me the bestest
birthday cake."

She waved her wand and there on the table appeared the biggest, gooiest, most scrummy cake you have ever seen.

"At last a spell that's worked! Now I'd better hurry and get ready,

the party will be starting soon."
Wanda decided to make a real
effort to look the best she could,
but without using any magic this
time! She had a bath, washed her
hair and even managed to brush it.
She put on a new sparkly blue
dress with gold moons, and a pair
of purple satin boots. She looked in
the mirror and smiled.

"I'm not so ugly after all," she
said to herself. "But I realise now
that being beautiful inside is more
important."

When she arrived at the party
everyone marvelled at the cake and
her friends told her how lovely she
looked. After Harry had opened all

of his presents he handed Wanda a parcel.

"But it's not my birthday," she said.

"I know. But we all wanted to buy you something to show you how much we love you," said Harry.

Wanda unwrapped the present and there inside was a wonderful new wand. "You won't get your

spells muddled now," laughed Harriet. Wanda thanked them all and felt very lucky to have so many friends. She spent the afternoon doing spells with her new wand, entertaining everyone at the party, and of course, eating lots of cake!

Monster Mayhem

Written by Claire Steeden

IN A GROUP OF CAVES, in the heart of a dark, dark forest, there once lived a collection of marvellous monsters. In one of the caves lived Rugged Red. He was terribly vain and spent nearly all day long looking at himself in the mirror. In fact, he did not have just one mirror, but hundreds of them. So wherever he turned he could see his reflection.

He loved his deep ruby red colour and told himself often how marvellous he looked. He was particularly proud of the smooth red spikes that stuck out all over his body.

Every day he would sit in his

cave, turning his head this way and that, admiring his reflection.

"Oh, you are so handsome," he would say to himself.

He would try all different sorts of hairstyles and pull a number of faces to see which expressions made him look his best.

Now, this in itself was bad enough, but all of Rugged's neighbours were exactly the same, if not worse. They all thought that they were the most handsome or beautiful monster in the world. As you can imagine, they were always arguing about who was the loveliest colour or who had the most attractive hairstyle.

Perfect Purple thought that her purple curls were absolutely fabulous. Brilliant blue, with his shiny scales, said that he was the most breathtaking monster of all. While Awesome Orange argued that his ringlets were the most remarkable of all.

Now, one day, Gorgeous Green, who was the Great Governor of the monsters, got fed up with listening to all the arguing and fighting, so she thought of a cunning plan to put a stop to it, once and for all. She decided to give a huge party and invite all the monsters. She made a long list and sent out posh invitations. Each one matched the colour of the monster she was inviting.

All the monsters were very excited. Wherever you went all you could hear were monsters arguing about who would look the best at the party. Even a few monsters that were not usually as vain as the others fell out with their friends.

The whole place buzzed with excitement. The hairdressers were busy. The Spike Specialists were fully booked. The Scale Scrapers were overrun with customers, not to mention the Claw Clippers and Fang Filers.

The air was filled with talk about colour and style, and size and

shape — what a hullabaloo. The
monsters argued and preened and
shouted and screamed until the
noise was unbearable.

When it was nearly time for the
party to start the monsters began
to queue outside the gates of
Gorgeous Green's garden. Together
they formed a rainbow of colours
— red, yellow, pink, green, orange,
purple and blue. It was a splendid
sight to see them all standing next
to each other.

At two o'clock the gates were
opened and the monsters filed in.
As they entered they were each
given a sparkling drink which
tasted very unusual. It kept

changing colour, and tiny coloured bubbles rose from the top.

Gorgeous Green had decorated her garden with balloons and streamers, and lots and lots of mirrors.

Finally, all the monsters arrived and the party got underway. There were long tables full of scrummy things to eat and a big bowl of punch, which looked delicious.

Gorgeous Green had organised party games and had hired a band to play all their favourite monster music.

It had all the ingredients of a perfect party, except for one thing. None of the monsters were interested in the food, the party games or the music. They were all much too busy looking at their reflections and arguing about who was the nicest colour.

Gorgeous Green had known that this would happen. She knew how unfriendly and vain all the monsters were and she was tired of seeing everyone so miserable. The monsters had forgotten how to have fun.

She stood on a platform and signalled to the band to stop playing. Then she spoke to the monsters.

"I have invited you to my party for a special reason. I have been watching and listening to you all for a long time. It makes me sad to see you fighting, especially when there is no reason to. You are all wonderful, and nobody is a nicer colour than anyone else."

With this all the monsters started talking at once. How could she say such a thing? It was ridiculous!

"Please listen. I invited you here to have fun and enjoy yourselves, but you are all too busy arguing. Well, I knew that talking to you wouldn't stop you from quarrelling, so I asked Wizzle the Wizard to make me a magic potion. As you came in you all drank a glass of his potion, and I'm glad to see that it has started to work. Go and look at yourselves in the mirrors."

With that, the monsters turned to look at their reflections, and guess what had happened!

Instead of seeing a blue monster, or a yellow monster in the mirror, they were grey. Every single monster had turned grey! They gasped and turned to Gorgeous Green in astonishment.

"I thought that if everyone looked the same, there would be nothing more to argue about. Now you can enjoy the party and have fun with your friends."

The monsters looked down at

themselves and then at each other. One by one they realised how silly they had been. All that time they had wasted when they could have been having fun.

The band started to play and Gorgeous Green, who was also grey by now, organised lots of games to play.

All the monsters had a wonderful afternoon. None of them could remember when they had had such a good time. They played, and danced and ate and laughed and sang. Gorgeous Green felt very happy. Her plan had worked. The monsters had stopped arguing at last.

Again she stood up to speak to them.

"This afternoon I think you've learnt a very important lesson. Now you can see that being a different colour doesn't matter. We are all friends because we like each other and nobody is better than anyone else. Since you have learnt your lesson, I think it's time to change back to our original colours. If you each have a glass of the punch on this table, you will turn back to the colour you were."

Everyone drank the punch and started to change back slowly. But this time they did not argue. They carried on with the party late into the night. Nobody wanted to go home, they all wanted to stay and have fun with their new found friends!